The RANDOM HOUSE Book of EASY·TO·READ STORIES

With an Introduction by Janet Schulman

RANDOM HOUSE  **NEW YORK**

Compilation and introduction copyright © 1993 by Random House, Inc.
Cover and title page art copyright © 1993 by Marc Brown. All rights
reserved under International and Pan-American Copyright Conventions.
Published in the United States by Random House, Inc., New York, and
simultaneously in Canada by Random House of Canada Limited, Toronto.

Library of Congress Cataloging-in-Publication Data:
The Random House book of easy-to-read stories.
    p.   cm.
SUMMARY: A collection of sixteen stories in easy-to-read format by such
authors as Dr. Seuss, Stan and Jan Berenstain, P. D. Eastman, and
Richard Scarry.
ISBN 0-679-83438-9 (trade); ISBN 0-679-93438-3 (lib. bdg.)
1. Children's stories, American. [1. Short stories.]
PZ5.R196   1993   [E]—dc20   92-40179

Manufactured in the United States of America
10 9 8 7 6 5 4 3 2

Copyright acknowledgments appear on pages 251 and 252.

Contents

A Note to Parents

One of the most magical moments in childhood is when children first see those funny little squiggles—otherwise known as letters—turn into words that they can actually read! *The Random House Book of Easy-to-Read Stories* has been compiled to help children make two important discoveries: first, that they *can* read, and second, that they *want* to read.

Some children are ready to read before they start school; others, not until they're seven or eight. And while a few children learn to read virtually by themselves, most need help and all need practice. Until four decades ago, the only practice children got was in school, with textbooks that drilled skills in as they drove joy out. Then, in 1957, something wonderful happened. Random House published *The Cat in the Hat* by Dr. Seuss—and suddenly learning to read became at-home fun!

Since that time, a whole body of easy-to-read books has been published. These books have short sentences and lots of lively pictures that are visual clues to the words and the action. Sometimes the illustrations make it possible for the child to read a hard, polysyllabic word, such as "dinosaur" or "astronaut." But usually the words have one or two syllables that can easily be sounded out. Some stories use rhyme and rhythm to help the fledgling reader. And of course, easy-to-read books always feature large type and plenty of space between lines.

But all of these learning-to-read aids are worthless without stories that have substance. Only stories that are rich in humor, feeling, or suspense can capture a child's interest and imagination. *The Random House Book of Easy-to-Read Stories* is a wonderful sampler of such stories. It provides hours of reading pleasure for beginning readers.

First try reading this book aloud to your child. The selections range from easy to more complex and include some Dr. Seuss tongue twisters that defy classification. Once familiar with the contents, a child will progress at his or her own pace—with encouragement from you. In no time, your child will be reading to *you* as, together, you lay the foundation for a lifetime of loving books!

—Janet Schulman, Publisher
Random House Books for Young Readers

Dog Party

BY P. D. EASTMAN

Now it is day.

The sun is up.

Now is the time

for all dogs to get up.

"Get up!"

It is day.

Time to get going.

Go, dogs. Go!

There they go.

Look at those dogs go!

Why are they going fast

in those cars?

What are they going to do?

Where are those dogs going?

Look where they are going.

They are all going to that

big tree over there.

Now the cars stop.

Now all the dogs get out.

And now look where

those dogs are going!

To the tree! To the tree!

Up the tree! Up the tree!

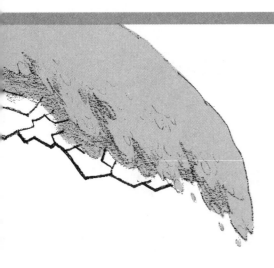

Up they go

to the top of the tree.

Why?

Will they work there?

Will they play there?

What is up there

on top of that tree?

A dog party!

A big dog party!

Big dogs, little dogs,

red dogs, blue dogs,

yellow dogs, green dogs,

black dogs, and white dogs

are all at a dog party!

What a dog party!

A Visit to Mr. Fixit

BY RICHARD SCARRY

Huckle Cat was so happy.

He had just bought

the perfect Mother's Day present.

A cuckoo-cuckoo clock!

"Mother will love it,"
he said.

"Cuckoo!" went the clock.

It was one o'clock.

He put the clock
into the basket of his bike.

Then he set off for home
as fast as he could go.

"Not so fast!" said Lowly Worm.

"Slow down!"

But Huckle did not slow down.

He turned the corner and
CRASHED

right into Postman Pig.

"Cucko-o-o-o-o!" went the clock.

Officer Murphy came right over.

"Oh, no! The clock is broken!"

said Huckle.

"You are lucky

that is all that is broken,"

said the police officer.

"You were going too fast.

And you did not ring

your bell."

Huckle said, "I'm sorry,

but my bell is broken."

Officer Murphy told Huckle

to get his bell fixed.

Huckle and Lowly went
to Mr. Fixit's store.
"Can you fix my bike bell
and this cuckoo-cuckoo clock?"
asked Huckle.
"Of course I can,"
said Mr. Fixit.
"Come back in an hour
and your bell and clock
will be as good as new."

Huckle and Lowly left the store.

Mr. Fixit set to work.

He took the bell apart.

He took the clock apart.

"Now, let me see . . ." he said.

When Huckle and Lowly came back,

Mr. Fixit had everything

back together again.

"Oh, thank you, Mr. Fixit!"

said Huckle.

"Glad to be of help,"

said Mr. Fixit.

Huckle could hardly wait
to give his mother the clock.
He got to his house
and rang his bike bell.
"Cuckoo-cuckoo!" went the bell.
Huckle was very surprised.

Cuckoo-cuckoo!

Then he gave the clock

to his mother.

"Happy Mother's Day," he said.

"Dring-dring!" went the clock.

Huckle was very surprised.

So was his mother.

"What a wonderful clock!"

she said.

"I have never seen

a cuckoo-cuckoo clock

that sounds like a bike bell!

Thank you so much, Huckle!"

Huckle loved

his new bike bell, too.

There was not another one

like it in Busytown!

He rushed off to thank

Mr. Fixit for the mixup.

And when he turned the corner,

he rang his bell.

"Cuckoo-cuckoo!"

Eat at Skipper Zipp's

BY DR. SEUSS

If you like to eat potato chips

and chew pork chops on clipper ships,

I suggest that you chew

a few chips and a chop

at Skipper Zipp's Clipper Ship Chip Chop Shop.

Mud

BY WENDY CHEYETTE LEWISON
ILLUSTRATED BY MARYANN COCCA-LEFFLER

Mud in the puddle. Mud on the shoe.

Mud on the socks. Mud on you.

Mud on your hands. Mud on your toes.

Mud on your cheeks. Mud on your nose.

Mud, mud, mud everywhere.

Mud on your elbows. Mud in your hair.

Mud on your chin. Mud on your ear.

Mud over there. Mud over here.

Mud in the puddle. Mud in the air.

Mud, mud, mud everywhere.

Mud!

The Teeny Tiny Woman

BY JANE O'CONNOR
ILLUSTRATED BY R. W. ALLEY

A teeny tiny woman
lived in a teeny tiny house.

One day she put on
her teeny tiny hat.

She got her teeny tiny bag.

And she went for

a teeny tiny walk.

Soon the teeny tiny woman
came to a teeny tiny gate.

She opened
the teeny tiny gate
and went into
a teeny tiny yard.

There she saw

a teeny tiny bone

on a teeny tiny grave.

"I can make some

teeny tiny soup

with this teeny tiny bone,"

said the teeny tiny woman.

The teeny tiny woman
put the teeny tiny bone
in her teeny tiny bag.

She went through
the teeny tiny gate
and walked home.

The teeny tiny woman

opened her teeny tiny door.

"My teeny tiny feet are tired,"
said the teeny tiny woman.

"I will not make
my teeny tiny soup now."

The teeny tiny woman
put the teeny tiny bone
in a teeny tiny cupboard.

Then she got into
her teeny tiny bed
for a teeny tiny nap.

Soon a teeny tiny
voice called:
"Give me my bone!"

The teeny tiny woman

was a teeny tiny bit scared.

"I must have had
a teeny tiny dream,"
she said.

The teeny tiny woman
had a teeny tiny glass
of milk.

Then she got back into
her teeny tiny bed.

Soon she fell asleep.

It was not long before
the teeny tiny voice
called out again.
"Give me my bone!"

The teeny tiny woman woke up.

She was so scared
she hid under
her teeny tiny covers.

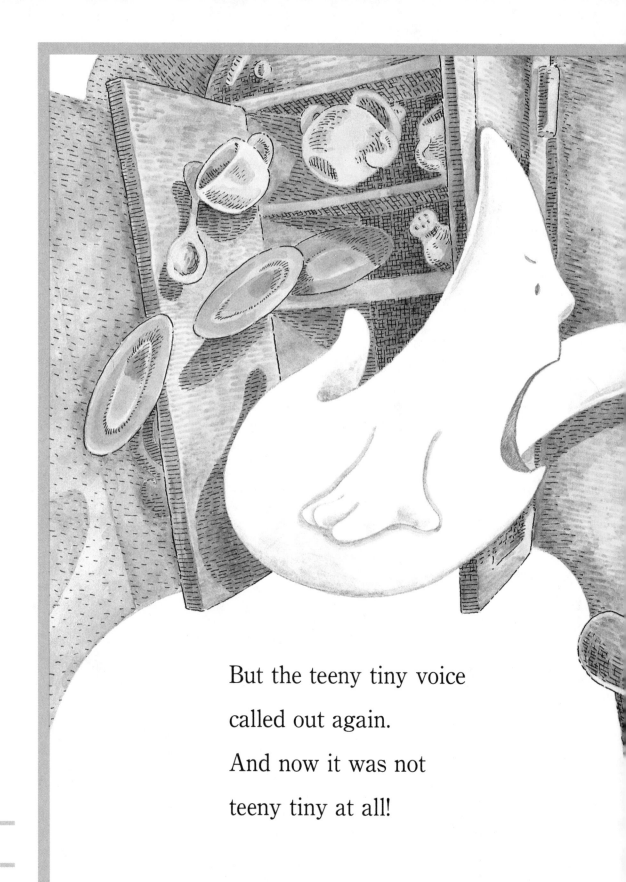

But the teeny tiny voice
called out again.
And now it was not
teeny tiny at all!

The teeny tiny woman
peeked out from under
her teeny tiny covers.

She said,

"TAKE IT!"

And that is the end of
this teeny tiny story.

The End

Babar's Picnic

BY LAURENT DE BRUNHOFF

"Let's have a picnic," says Babar.

"A picnic!" says Celeste.

"I will find the perfect spot."

Babar and Celeste go to the garden.

"No, no, no," says Celeste.

"I do not see the perfect spot.

But I do see Cornelius!"

"A picnic!" says Cornelius.

"I will find the perfect spot."

They all go to the park.

"No, no, no," says Cornelius.

"I do not see the perfect spot.

But I do see Zephir and Arthur!"

"A picnic!" say Zephir and Arthur.

"We will find the perfect spot."

They all go to the beach.

"No, no, no," say Zephir and Arthur.

"We do not see the perfect spot.

But we do see the Old Lady and the children!"

"A picnic!" says the Old Lady.

"We will find the perfect spot."

They all go back to the garden.

"Hooray!" says Celeste.

"This is the perfect spot after all."

The Surprise Party

BY ANNABELLE PRAGER

ILLUSTRATED BY TOMIE DE PAOLA

"Know what?" said Nicky.

"No, what?" said Albert.

"My birthday is coming,"
 Nicky told Albert.

"I am going to have
 a birthday party."

"Great!" said Albert.

"Are you going to invite me?"

"Of course I am going to invite you,"
 said Nicky.

He took out his list.

"I'm going to invite you and Ann,

and Jenny and Jan,

and Morris and Doris,

and Dan."

"That sure is a lot of people,"

said Albert.

"You have to have a lot of people
at a birthday party,"
said Nicky.
"That way you get a lot of presents.
Come on. I need you to help me."
Albert and Nicky
went to Nicky's house.

Nicky took out his bank.

He shook it upside down.

Out fell a quarter and two dimes.

"Oh, no," he said.

"This is not enough money

for a party."

"What are you going to do?"

said Albert.

"I'll think of something,"

said Nicky.

Suddenly his face broke into a smile.

"I know," he said.

"I'll have a surprise party."

"A surprise party for who?"

asked Albert.

"A surprise party for me," said Nicky.

The next day Albert and Nicky

met at the playground.

"I've been thinking," said Albert.

"You can't give a surprise party

for yourself.

You won't be surprised."

"Of course I can't give

a surprise party for myself,"

said Nicky. "But YOU can.

You and Ann, and Jenny and Jan,

and Morris and Doris, and Dan."

"How are we going to do that?"

asked Albert.

Nicky started swinging on a swing.

"Easy," said Nicky. "You say—

Listen, you guys.

Nicky's birthday is coming.

Let's give him a surprise party.

"Then they'll say—

What a good idea.

We love surprise parties.

Albert can bring the cake.

Ann can bring the ice cream.

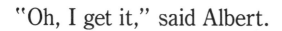

Jenny can bring the…"

"Oh, I get it," said Albert.

"Everyone will bring something.

What a good idea."

Nicky and Albert

started out of the playground.

"You can get the party ready

at my house.

I will be out

having my tuba lesson,"

Nicky said.

"When I come home you will yell

SURPRISE!

Know what, Albert?

I'll be very surprised

if this doesn't turn out to be

the best surprise party

that ever was."

Albert ran home to call up Ann,

and Jenny and Jan,

and Morris and Doris,

and Dan.

Sure enough, they all said,

"What a good idea!

We love surprise parties."

They all met at Albert's house
to plan the party.

"We can fix the party
at Nicky's house,"
Albert said.
"He will be out
having his tuba lesson.
When he comes home
we will yell SURPRISE!"
Just then the telephone rang.
Albert answered it.
"Hello," he said.

It was Nicky.

"I forgot to tell you something,"
said Nicky.

"I love balloons
with HAPPY BIRTHDAY on them."

"Okay," said Albert nervously.

"Good-bye."

"Who was that?" asked Ann.

Albert thought very fast.

"Uh…that was my Aunt Belinda,"

he said.

"Shall we have balloons

with HAPPY BIRTHDAY on them?"

"Yes, yes, yes!" shouted everyone.

Ting-a-ling-a-ling.

The phone rang again.

Albert answered it again.

It was Nicky again.

"Can we have snappers?"

asked Nicky.

"The kind that go bang

when you pull them?"

"Sure, Aunt Belinda," said Albert.

Albert slammed down the phone.

He turned to the group.

"Shall we have snappers?" he asked.

"Do you mean the kind that go bang

when you pull them?" said Jenny.

"They're so scary. I love them."

Ting-a-ling-a-ling.

"Let me answer it," said Jan.

"No, no, no!" cried Albert.

He grabbed the phone.

It was Nicky again.

"Be sure that everyone

brings a present," said Nicky.

"And remember

my favorite color is blue."

"Of course, Aunt Belinda,"

said Albert.

"GOOD-BYE!"

"Why does your aunt call you

every five minutes?"

asked Morris and Doris.

"My Aunt Belinda is very lonely,"

said Albert.

"Now, let me think," said Albert.

"Nicky's favorite color is blue.

I am going to make

a beautiful blue birthday cake."

"Do we have to bring

a present?" asked Dan.

"Of course," said Albert.

"Everyone has to bring a present.

Oh, boy, will Nicky be surprised!"

The next day

Nicky and Albert

were roller-skating in the park.

"It will be awful

if anyone finds out

that I know about the party!"

said Nicky.

"Shush," said Albert.
"Here comes Ann
   on her pogo stick."
   Nicky gave a little smile.
"I'd better make sure
   that Ann doesn't think
   I know about the party,"
   he said.

Ann stopped hopping.

"Hi," she said.

"Hi, Ann," said Nicky.

"Guess what I am doing

on my birthday."

Ann gave Albert a worried look.

"What?" she asked.

"My tuba teacher is taking me

to a concert," said Nicky.

"Oh, NO," said Ann.

"Why do you say Oh, NO?"
asked Nicky.

"Don't you like concerts?"

"What I meant to say," said Ann,

"was, Oh, no—no kidding. Excuse me.
I have to go and see Jenny and Jan,
and Morris and Doris, and Dan."

Ann got on her pogo stick

and hopped away

as fast as she could.

Nicky laughed and laughed.

"I fooled her," he said.

"Now nobody can possibly think

that I know about the party.

Oh, I can't wait

for my birthday to come."

Three days later

Nicky was walking home

from his tuba lesson.

It was his birthday.

He gave a little skip of excitement.

The day of the party

had finally come!

When Nicky got

to his little house,

it was all dark.

His heart was going

thump thump thump.

"I'd better act very surprised,"

thought Nicky.

"Or everyone will think

I know about the party."

He practiced making

a surprised face.

Then he opened his front door
very slowly.

Nothing happened.

He went into his living room
very slowly.

Nothing happened.

He turned on the light.

Nobody was there.

"Where's the party?" he wondered.

"Oh, I bet they are hiding."

He waited and waited.

Nothing happened.

All of a sudden

the doorbell rang.

"There they are!"

he thought happily.

He practiced making

more surprised faces

on the way to the door.

It was Albert, all alone.

"Where is my party?"

shouted Nicky.

"Oh, Nicky," said Albert.

"It is awful.

Ann told everyone

that you were going to a concert

with your tuba teacher.

So they called off the party."

"Oh, my," cried Nicky.

"Oh, my beautiful surprise party."

A big tear ran down his cheek.

"Don't feel too bad,"

Albert said.

"They are going to have the party

on your next birthday.

You can look forward to it

for twelve whole months."

"I should never have played a trick
on my friends," cried Nicky.
"Never mind," said Albert.
"I made a cake for you anyway.
Come to my house and we can eat it."

They walked to Albert's house.

Albert opened his front door.

Nicky went in.

Albert turned on the light.

"SURPRISE! SURPRISE!"
shouted Ann,
and Jenny and Jan,
and Morris and Doris,
and Dan.

Nicky looked all around him.

There were balloons

with HAPPY BIRTHDAY on them.

There was a table

with a blue paper tablecloth

and blue paper plates.

By each plate

there was a red snapper

and a little basket of candy.

Best of all,

there was a pile of presents.

Each one was tied with a big bow.

And each one had a surprise inside.

"Wow!" said Nicky.

"Know what?"

said Albert.

"No, what?"

said Nicky.

"You said you wanted
    the best surprise party that ever was,"
said Albert.
"So we made it a surprise!"

The Prince Has a Boo-boo

BY Harriet Ziefert

ILLUSTRATED BY R. W. Alley

A little prince played in the castle.

The little prince bumped his head.

"I have a boo-boo! I need a Band-Aid," he cried.

"The prince bumped his head.

He needs a Band-Aid," cried the nanny.

"The prince needs a Band-Aid," cried the cook.

"The prince needs a Band-Aid," cried the king.

"The prince needs a Band-Aid," cried the queen.

"I'll get the Band-Aid," said the general.

"Here is the Band-Aid," said the general.

He gave it to the queen.

The queen gave it to the king.

The king gave it to the cook.

The cook gave it to the nanny.

"Here is the Band-Aid," said the nanny.

"Thank you," said the prince.

"Now kiss my boo-boo

and make it better."

Inside, Outside, Upside Down
BY STAN AND JAN BERENSTAIN

Going in

Inside

THIS SIDE UP

Inside a box

Upside down

Inside a box

Upside down

Going out

Outside

Outside

Inside a box

Upside down

Going on

On a truck

Outside

Inside a box

Upside down

Going

Going to town

On a truck

Outside

Inside a box

Upside down

Falling off

Off the truck

Coming out

Right side up!

Tweetle Beetles

BY Dr. Seuss

What do you know

about tweetle beetles?

Well…

When tweetle beetles fight,

it's called

a tweetle beetle battle.

And when they

battle in a puddle,

it's a tweetle

beetle puddle battle.

AND when tweetle beetles

battle with paddles in a puddle,

they call it a tweetle

beetle puddle paddle battle.

AND...

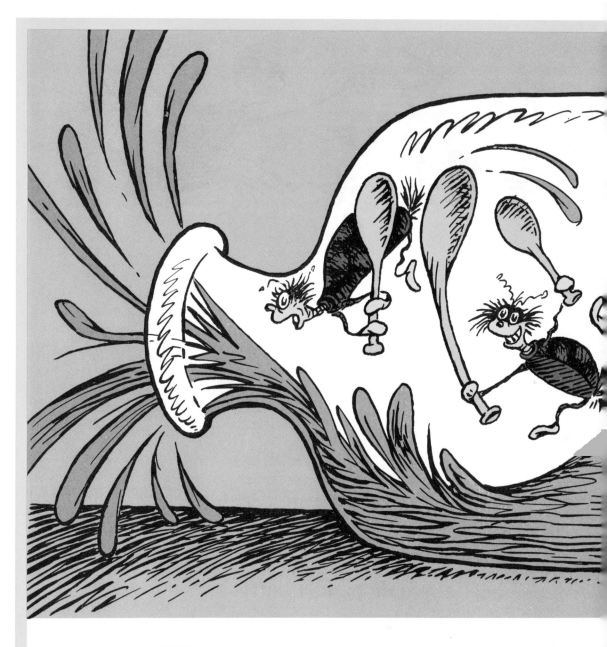

When beetles battle beetles

in a puddle paddle battle

and the beetle battle puddle

is a puddle in a bottle...

...they call this

a tweetle beetle

bottle puddle

paddle battle muddle.

AND...

When beetles
fight these battles
in a bottle
with their paddles
and the bottle's
on a poodle
and the poodle's
eating noodles…

…they call this

a muddle puddle

tweetle poodle

beetle noodle

bottle paddle battle.

AND…

When a fox is
in the bottle where
the tweetle beetles battle
with their paddles
in a puddle on a
noodle-eating poodle,
THIS is what they call...

...a tweetle beetle

noodle poodle bottled

paddled muddled duddled

fuddled wuddled

fox in socks, sir!

Freddie's Spaghetti

BY CHARLOTTE DOYLE

ILLUSTRATED BY NICHOLAS REILLY

"What's for dinner, Mommy?" said Freddie.

Freddie's mommy said, "Spaghetti."

"Wow! Spaghetti!" said Freddie. "I'm ready."

Freddie's mommy said, "The spaghetti

isn't ready. You have to wait."

Freddie sat on his hands and said,

"I don't know how to wait."

"We can help you wait," said the blocks.

"We can help you build."

Build, Freddie, build.

"We can help you wait," said the drums.

"We can help you march."

March, Freddie, march.

"I can help you wait," said the rocking horse.

"You can have a ride."

Ride, Freddie, ride.

Freddie's mommy said to Freddie,

"Freddie, the spaghetti's ready."

Freddie washed his hands,

sat on his chair, and WOW!

A great big bowl of spaghetti—

all for Freddie!

Freddie ate spaghetti,

and Freddie ate spaghetti,

and Freddie ate spaghetti,

till it was all gone.

Little Witch's Big Night

BY DEBORAH HAUTZIG

ILLUSTRATED BY MARC BROWN

It was Halloween night.

All the witches were busy.

They were busy getting ready

for their Halloween ride.

Grouchy Witch was busy
making grouchy faces
in her cracked mirror.

Nasty Witch was busy
shooting a water gun
at her cat, Bow-Wow.

Mother Witch was busy
making a new broomstick
for Little Witch.

Oh, what a wonderful Halloween
it was going to be!

All the witches were ready…

but where was Little Witch?

"Little Witch, what are you doing?"

called Mother Witch.

Mother Witch went upstairs
and into Little Witch's room.
"What! You made your bed again!"
screeched Mother Witch.
"Sorry, Mother. I forgot,"
said Little Witch.

Then Mother Witch looked
under the bed.
"And you cleaned your cobwebs!"
Mother Witch was angry.

"You really must be punished.
You will stay home tonight
while we go flying,"
said Mother Witch.
"But it is Halloween!"
said Little Witch.

"Maybe this will teach you
not to be so good,"
said Mother Witch.

Little Witch watched
the big witches fly off.
Oh, how she wanted
to fly with them!
She was very sad.

Her bat, Scrubby,

wanted to cheer her up.

He made funny faces...

and he did silly tricks.

"Even my bat is good!"

cried Little Witch.

"This is the worst Halloween ever."

Suddenly—

ding, dong went the doorbell.

Little Witch ran to the door.

She opened it and saw

a devil,

a pirate,

and an astronaut.

Each had a big bag of candy.

"Trick or treat!"

they said.

"Oh, dear," said Little Witch.

"I have no treats for you."

"No treats!" said the devil.

"No treats!" said the pirate.

"No treats!" said the astronaut.

"But it is Halloween!"

said the three trick-or-treaters.

They started to walk away.

"Wait," said Little Witch.

"Maybe I can

give you a treat."

"I can give you a ride

on my broomstick,"

she said.

"Really?" said the devil.

"Wow!" said the pirate.

"Can you really fly?"

asked the astronaut.

"Just wait and see!"

said Little Witch proudly.

"But there is room for just two

on my broomstick."

The devil said, "Me first!"

Little Witch sat in front.

She said some magic words:

"Horrible borrible,

Spinach pie,

Come on, broomstick,

Fly, fly, fly!"

WHOOSH! The broomstick

shot off the porch

and up into the sky.

Up and up they flew.

The houses and trees looked

like little toys.

Little Witch said

more magic words:

    "Bibbety boppety,

    Lizard soup,

    Broomstick, do a

    Loop-the-loop!"

The broomstick did
a perfect loop-the-loop.

"Wow!" said the devil.
"You really are
a wonderful witch!"
"Thank you,"
said Little Witch.
"And now...

"Alakazoo,

Four-leaf clover,

Back we fly—

Your turn is over."

THUMP! The broomstick landed

back on the porch.

Next it was the pirate's turn.

"Hold on tight!"

said Little Witch.

And with another big WHOOSH

they zoomed into the sky.

Soon they were flying
over the ocean.
Below them was
a real pirate ship!

The pirate captain looked up.

He did not believe

what he saw.

"Shiver me timbers!

A witch and a flying pirate!"

he shouted.

Little Witch and her friend

waved to the pirate captain.

"Now we will fly home—

backward!"

said Little Witch.

She said the magic words:

"Mumbo jumbo,

Broomy stick,

Take us home—

And make it quick!"

They zoomed backward,

over the ocean,

over the town,

and back to Little Witch's porch.

"Now it is my turn!"

said the astronaut.

She got onto the broomstick

and Little Witch said:

"Hocus-pocus,

Peanut stew,

Here's a broomstick

Ride for you!"

And—WHOOSH—they were off.

Little Witch and the astronaut
flew over the big city.
They whizzed around
the tall buildings.

They saw jack-o'-lanterns
in the windows.
The jack-o'-lanterns winked
at them.
Little Witch and the astronaut
winked right back.

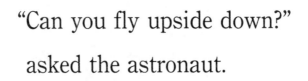

"Can you fly upside down?"
asked the astronaut.
"Yes, I can!"
said Little Witch,
and she said the magic words:
  "Harum-scarum,
  Witches' vats,
  Now we're hanging
  Just like bats!"

Flip-flop!

Upside down they flew

over the roofs and past the moon.

Then the broomstick took them back
to Little Witch's porch.
The three trick-or-treaters
clapped their hands.
"This was the best Halloween yet!"
they said.
"Let's go flying next year too!"
Little Witch smiled.
"That's a good idea,"
she said.

"Well, good-bye," said the devil,
the pirate, and the astronaut.
"And thank you!"

Little Witch waved good-bye
to her friends.

Then she swept the porch.

"I will be very good all year,"
she told Scrubby.

"Then Mother will punish me
and I can fly again
with my new friends."

Little Witch was reading
a bedtime story to Scrubby
when the big witches came home.

Grouchy Witch said,

"You missed the spookiest

Halloween ever!"

Nasty Witch said,

"We scared all the children!"

Mother Witch said,

"I hope you learned

your lesson."

"Because," said Mother Witch,

"I learned MY lesson.

Halloween is not fun

without you.

I missed you, Little Witch!"

Then she gave Little Witch
a big Halloween hug.

At bedtime Mother Witch told
Little Witch a spooky story.

Then she tucked her in.
"Next year you can fly
with us. I promise,"
said Mother Witch.
"Can I bring some friends?"
asked Little Witch.
"Yes—if you promise
not to be too good,"
said Mother Witch.

"I will do my best, Mother,"
said Little Witch.
And she really meant it.
Then Little Witch fell asleep
and dreamed about
the best Hallowen ever.

The Ugly Duckling

ADAPTED BY KATHARINE ROSS

ILLUSTRATED BY BERNHARD OBERDIECK

Once upon a time, some ducklings hatched.

"You are not like the others," said the mama.

"You are an ugly one," said the mama.

"Ugly duckling! Ugly duckling!" said the others.

The ugly duckling ran away.

"Why am I so ugly?"

the ugly duckling asked the lake.

"Who knows?" said the lake.

"Why am I so ugly?"

the ugly duckling asked the wild ducks.

"Who knows?" said the wild ducks.

"Why am I so ugly?"

the ugly duckling asked the dog.

The dog ran away!

"Why can't I be beautiful like the swans?"

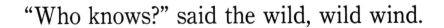

"Who knows?" said the wild, wild wind.

"Who knows why you are so ugly?" said the man.

"But my children like ducklings."

"Ugly duckling! Ugly duckling!" said the children.

The ugly duckling ran away.

The ugly duckling grew…

and grew… and grew!

"Why can't I be beautiful like you?"

said the ugly duckling.

"But you *are* beautiful," said the swans.

"Am I beautiful?" asked the ugly duckling.

"Yes," said the lake.

"Yes," said the dog.

"Yes," said the children.

"Yes, yes, yes!" said the wild, wild wind.

"You are a beautiful swan."

Why did a swan hatch

with some ducklings?

Who knows!

The Fuddnuddlers

BY DR. SEUSS

There are so many things

that you really should know.

And that's why I'm bothering telling you so.

You should know the first names

of the Fuddnuddler Brothers

who like to pile each on the heads of others.

If you start at the top,

there are Bipper and Bud

and Skipper and Jipper

and Jeffrey and Jud,

Horatio, Horace and Hendrix and Hud,

and then come Dinwoodie and Dinty and Dud,

also Fitzsimmon and Frederick and Fud,

and Slinkey and Stinkey and Stuart and Stud.

And, down at the bottom is poor little Lud.

But if Lud ever sneezes, his name will be MUD.

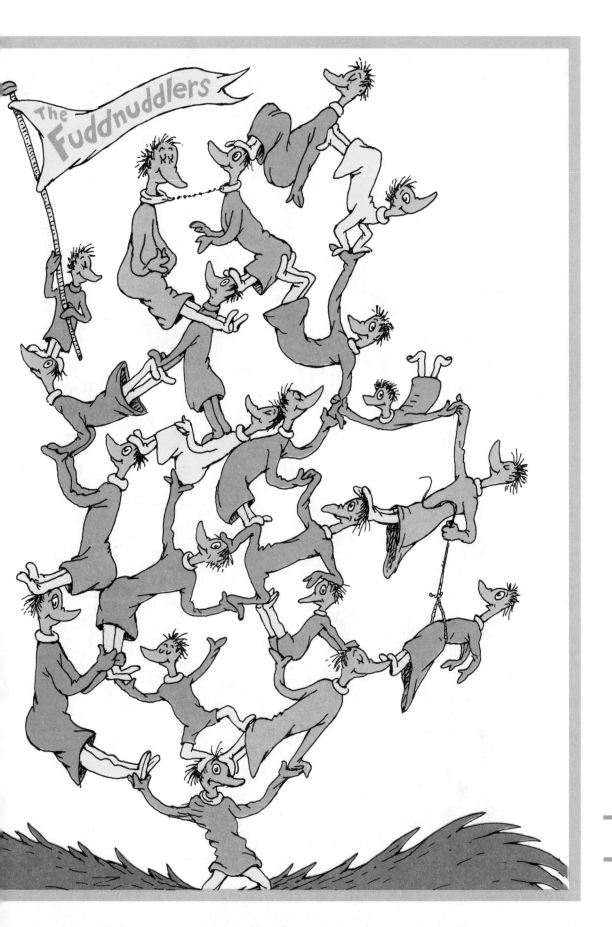

20,000 Baseball Cards Under the Sea

BY JON BULLER AND SUSAN SCHADE

I'm a collector.

I collect baseball cards, dinosaurs, comic books, robots, and cars.

My friend Kenneth is a collector too.

One day I was going to visit Kenneth after school.

I was dreaming about what I could buy if I won the lottery. Would I buy a Corvette, a Rolls-Royce, or a Jeep?

I wasn't looking where I was going.

Yikes! I almost stepped on a big black snake! At least it looked like a snake. But it was nothing but an old strip of rubber.

I decided to give it to Kenneth. He would find a use for it.

What Kenneth collects is junk. He
likes to make stuff out of it.
Kenneth is into recycling.

He was really happy when I brought
him the strip of rubber.

"I can use that," he said, and he hung
it over a hook.

We went into the kitchen.

Kenneth always makes me fish cakes with maple syrup. He knows how much I like them. He likes them too.

"So, Roger, how was school today?" he asked me.

I always tell him about my troubles in school. "I was the last kid picked for basketball," I said. "Even after the girls. And the lunch was ravioli."

Then Kenneth tells me about his troubles.

"Do you know they raised my taxes to $2,000? Where am I going to get $2,000? This country is in bad shape. In fact, this whole planet is a mess."

After we ate we went outside.
Kenneth brought the strip of rubber and
we went to look at his latest project.

It looked like a giant pill on wheels. Kenneth started gluing the rubber around the front end. "This strip is just what I needed for the door," he said.

When he was done, he opened the door and climbed in. "Come on, Roger," he said, "let's try her out!"

I had never tried any of Kenneth's contraptions before.

I wasn't sure I wanted to. But I crawled inside anyway.

Kenneth turned a key. The whole contraption rattled and shook. We started moving out of Kenneth's backyard and onto the beach.

Uh-oh! We were headed right for the water.

We went into the water.

We went UNDER the water!

I was under the sea in a homemade submarine.

A little stream of brownish water bubbled through a crack in the wall.

"Uh, Kenneth." I touched his sleeve
and pointed to the leak.

"No problem," he said, handing me a
jar. "Slap some of this gunk on there, will
you?"

I slapped some of the gunk on it, and
the leak stopped.

Then I looked out the window. It was beautiful! We were cruising above the ocean floor. The scenery was awesome.

Light rays rippled through the water. Plants swayed back and forth. A mermaid swam past the window. A MERMAID?

"Hey!" I cried. "That was a . . ."

"I know," Kenneth said. "Lots of them down here."

I kept looking. He was right.

After a while we ran right into a
rocky wall and stopped.

"Uh-oh!" I said.

"Uh-oh, nothing," said Kenneth. "This
is where we get out."

He opened the door.

"Hey!" I cried. I expected a big flood, but nothing happened. The rubber strip made a tight seal against the wall.

We were looking at another door. It was fitted into the rock wall.

Kenneth opened it, and we crawled
into an underwater cavern.

It was full of junk! "How do you like
my storage shed?" Kenneth asked me.

I was speechless.

"Where does all this stuff come from?"
I finally asked. "How did it get here?"

"It comes from old shipwrecks. The
merpeople collect it for me. And I make
things for them. We have a nice
arrangement."

I looked out the window. Some of the merpeople were driving by in funny contraptions. I recognized Kenneth's work.

"Have a look around, Roger," he said. "Let me know if you see anything you want."

OH BOY!

There was a lot of neat stuff. Hats and boots and fishhooks. And towels and books and big ropes and diving gear. And propellers and broken chairs and a tuba.

There were ships' instruments made
of polished wood with gears and dials. I
wasn't sure what they were for, but I
liked them a lot.

In one corner there were some old books and magazines piled up on a big wooden trunk. They were all dusty.

I moved the books and magazines and opened the trunk.

It was full of unopened packs of baseball cards! I had found something I wanted all right.

I opened one of the packs.

The bubble gum was pretty stale. But the top card was the 1951 Tony Pudnik rookie card!

Can you believe it?

In my baseball-card catalog there's a whole page on that card. It's worth $5,000! No kidding.

I almost swallowed my gum.

I was counting out the packs and scratching numbers in the sand when Kenneth called me.

"Hey, Roger!"

"Just give me five more minutes!" I shouted.

"Five minutes?" said Kenneth. "You can have fifty years! We're staying!"

"Staying? You mean underwater? FOREVER?"

"Why not?" said Kenneth. "Think about it. No more taxes! No more worries. Mermaids. Plenty of junk. No more school."

No school. That did make me think. Except . . .

"Are there other kids down here?" I asked.

"Sure," said Kenneth. "Merkids!"

He waved his hand toward the porthole. A mermaid girl was swimming by.

She saw me. She called her friend over. They were both looking at me and pointing and laughing.

I danced the hokey-pokey for them.
They loved it.

I was thinking maybe it would be okay to live underwater for a while. Of course I would have to call my mother.

Then I remembered the baseball cards.

"Oh heck," I said. "I was going to sell some of these cards and buy a Corvette."

Kenneth laughed and laughed.

"No, really," I said. "Don't you know
what these are worth? Tony Pudnik is
going for $5,000! And you could probably
get $1,500 for this one, maybe $2,000.
You've got about 20,000 cards here, and
even if they sold for only $10 apiece, that
would be $200,000!"

Kenneth looked sort of excited.

"You've got a lot of valuable stuff
down here," I said. "These old comics are
worth a lot too."

"So I could pay my taxes," he said
slowly.

"No problem," I said.

"I could keep my house and still visit
the merpeople," said Kenneth. "Okay,
we'll go fifty-fifty."

I thought that was pretty generous.
We shook hands on it.

So that's how I got my Corvette.

Of course, I don't have my license yet. But sometimes I let my mother drive me around.

46

And I still have the Tony Pudnik rookie card, too.

Some things are worth more than money.

I Can Read
with My Eyes Shut

BY DR. SEUSS

Young cat! If you keep
your eyes open enough,
oh, the stuff you will learn!
The most wonderful stuff!

You'll learn about…

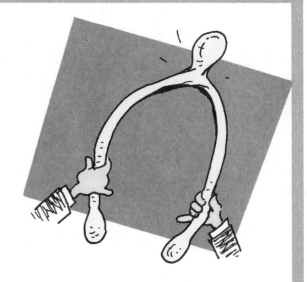

fishbones...   and wishbones.

You'll learn about trombones, too.

You'll learn
about Jake
the Pillow Snake.

and all about
Foo-Foo the Snoo.

You can learn about ice.

You can learn about mice.

Mice on ice.

And
ice
on
mice.

You can learn about
the price of ice.

Nice ice
for sale.
Ten cents a pail.

You can learn about SAD.....

and GLAD...

and MAD!

There are
so many things
you can learn about.
BUT...you'll miss
the best things
if you keep
your eyes shut.

OUT

IN

The more that you read,

the more things you will know.

The more that you learn,

the more places you'll go.

ACKNOWLEDGMENTS

Babar's Picnic by Laurent de Brunhoff. Copyright © 1991 by Laurent de Brunhoff. Reprinted by permission of Random House, Inc.

"A Visit to Mr. Fixit" from *The Best Mistake Ever! and Other Stories* by Richard Scarry. Copyright © 1984 by Richard Scarry. Reprinted by permission of Random House, Inc.

"Tweetle Beetles" from *Fox in Socks* by Dr. Seuss. Copyright © 1965 by Theodor S. Geisel and Audrey S. Geisel. Copyright renewed 1993 by Audrey S. Geisel. Reprinted by permission of Random House, Inc.

Freddie's Spaghetti by Charlotte Doyle, illustrated by Nicholas Reilly. Text copyright © 1991 by Charlotte Doyle. Illustrations copyright © 1991 by Nicholas Reilly. Reprinted by permission of Random House, Inc.

"Dog Party" from *Go, Dog. Go!* by P. D. Eastman. Copyright © 1961 by P. D. Eastman. Copyright renewed 1989 by Mary L. Eastman. Reprinted by permission of Random House, Inc.

Excerpt from *I Can Read with My Eyes Shut!* by Dr. Seuss. Copyright © 1978 by Theodor S. Geisel and Audrey S. Geisel. Reprinted by permission of Random House, Inc.

Inside, Outside, Upside Down by Stan and Jan Berenstain. Copyright © 1968 by Stanley and Janice Berenstain. Reprinted by permission of Random House, Inc.

Little Witch's Big Night by Deborah Hautzig, illustrated by Marc Brown. Text copyright © 1984 by Random House, Inc. Illustrations copyright © 1984 by Marc Brown. Reprinted by permission of Random House, Inc.

Mud by Wendy Cheyette Lewison, illustrated by Maryann Cocca-Leffler. Text copyright © 1990 by Wendy Cheyette Lewison. Illustrations copyright © 1990 by Maryann Cocca-Leffler. Reprinted by permission of Random House, Inc.

"Eat at Skipper Zipp's" and "The Fuddnuddlers" from *Oh Say Can You Say?* by Dr. Seuss. Copyright © 1979 by Theodor S. Geisel and Audrey S. Geisel. Reprinted by permission of Random House, Inc.

Continued on next page